MW01017215

Lucky Me

A Children's Guide to Animal Companionship and Safety

Written and Photographed by

Christi Drue Dunlap

Dedication

For Scratch and Sophie Jane.
Thank you for indulging my love of animals and welcoming them
into our home, despite your best judgment.

My Promise to My New Animal Friend

I, _____, promise to always take care of my new
 (child's name)

animal friend, _____. I will provide him/her with
 (animal's name)

food, water, shelter and love. I will always keep him/her safe.

Signed,

_____
 (child's signature)

Many of us love the idea of bringing home a new companion animal to be part of our family. Not all of us understand that this is a very big undertaking. You not only want to find the right animal for your family, you also need to be able to provide for his needs and keep him safe. This is a big commitment.

Join a dog named Rocky as he and his friends guide us through what a humane society can offer to animals, and what every animal guardian should know about caring for and keeping their new family member safe.

Every animal has a story to tell…

Hi, my name is Rocket.
But you can call me Rocky.

Everyone does.

There is a lot to know before you bring a new animal friend home to live with you.

My friends and I have some things we'd like to share.

A long time ago, I was roaming around on the streets and was picked up by an animal control officer.

When she found me, I was very hungry and cold.

Some call her "the dog catcher" and think it's a bad thing, but she saved my life.

I am a very lucky dog.

She brought me to the Humane Society.

They gave me something to eat, drink and a warm place to sleep.

I was pretty sick when I arrived at the Humane Society and needed care from a veterinarian, just like my friend Harry here.

A veterinarian is an animal doctor who gives us care and medicine to help us get better when we are sick.

I also had an operation so I can't make any puppies. There are already so many dogs (and other animals) that need homes, that it is important to have this operation.

There are many wonderful people who help take care of the animals at the Humane Society.

They bring us blankets, fresh water and food every day.

They socialize us too. That means they play with us, and make sure we are used to being around people.

Animals and people speak different languages. Sometimes we need to learn that people are friendly and loving by interacting with them.

When I was no longer sick, I was put up for adoption. That means that they helped me find my new home.

I was so happy.

Did you know animals have feelings? Speaking for myself and my animal friends, I can tell you we definitely do.

By just looking at us, you can often tell how we are feeling. Remember, animals use their whole bodies as well as their voices to let you know.

Oliver purrs to tell you he likes how you are petting him.

Durham shouldn't be bothered while he is eating. He might growl to let you know he doesn't want to play right now.

Gherkin hisses when she is nervous and doesn't want to be touched.

My friend Puck wags his tail to show you he is happy and ready to play.

We animals need a few things when we come to live with you. My new family made sure that I had everything I needed.

Can you think of what would make us feel welcome and safe in our new home?

Food and a bowl of my own, so I know I can eat whatever is in it without being scolded.

Fresh water is important to us animals.

If someone left a big glass of water out on the counter for a week, would you want to drink it? Me neither!

Having a bed of my own makes me feel secure.

Our own toys will help keep us out of things we shouldn't play with (like your toys and shoes!).

If we can't be with you, please leave us with something safe to play with.

We also need lots of love and attention. It's important to spend time with us every day.

There are many ways you can help keep us
safe when we come home to live with you.

Can you think of some?

Puck likes to go for walks, but to do so he needs to be on a leash. Whenever we are outside of your yard, make sure you keep us on a leash.

This keeps us safe from getting lost, being hit by a car, getting in fights or catching diseases from other animals.

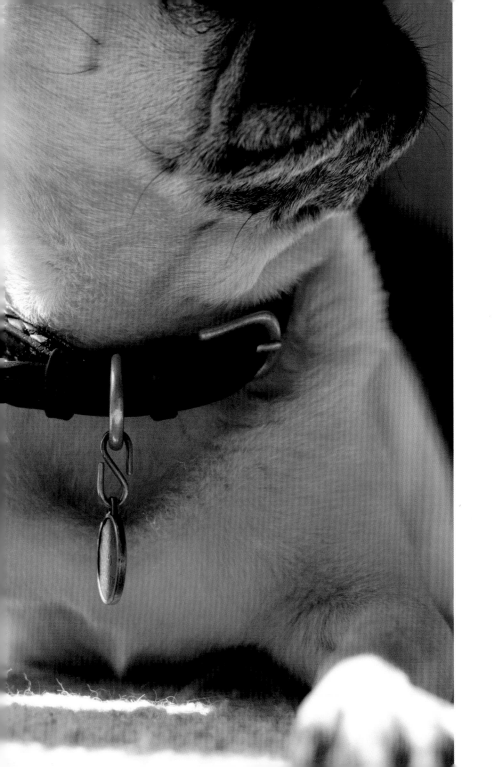

A collar with identification tags, including a phone number, will help others reach you if we get lost.

You should also license your dog or cat. This is required by most local governments, and helps the Humane Society locate you if we should get lost. Your animal friend must have a rabies shot before getting a license. This helps all of us stay healthier and safer.

To keep yourself safe, you should be careful when you see an unfamiliar dog, even if he looks friendly like my buddy Bogart.

The first thing you should always do is tell a grownup – a teacher, a parent, or anyone else you know.

It is best not to approach to try to read the identification tags; let a grownup do that.

If a loose dog comes toward you, you can act like a tree or, if you are already down on the ground, act like a rock. Trees and rocks don't talk or move. The dog should get bored and move on.

We dogs like to chase! All dogs, even a short one
like me, can run faster than you can.

Never run from a dog you don't know.

My friend Belle doesn't know you and she might get nervous if you stare at her.

Don't look an unfamiliar dog directly in the eye. She may think you are a bully and trying to hurt her.

It is safest for cats to be kept inside your home. This way they won't get lost, chased or hurt.

Don't stick your fingers in cages occupied by animals.

Remember the "do's" and "don'ts" of greeting a dog with his or her owner.

Always ask permission. "May I pet your dog?"

If the owner says "No," respect their answer and don't take it personally.

The dog may not like children, or may be having a tough day.

If the owner says "Yes," curl your fingers into a soft fist and slowly offer the back of your hand to the dog to sniff.

Let the dog smell the back of your hand.

This is like a handshake for a dog.

After you have introduced yourself, you can pet the dog gently.

Not all dogs like to be pet on the head, so pet them on the back.

Having an animal friend in your life can be a lot of fun!

It is also a very big commitment.

Remember, there are lots of things we need: food, water, shelter, love…

If you do decide to have an animal friend join your family, I hope you will look for him or her at the Humane Society like my family did for me!

Rocky,
Pug

Martha,
Bernese Mountain Dog

Bogart,
Vizsla

Belle,
Lewellen Setter

Durham,
*Great Dane/American
Pit Bull Mix*

Oliver,
Domestic Long-Hair

Gherkin,
Domestic Short-Hair

Puck,
Cairn Terrier Mix

Harry,
Poodle/Bichon Frise Mix

Serena,
Calico Domestic Short-Hair

Resources

Find your local humane society:
www.pets911.com

Volunteer at your local animal shelter:
www.hsus.org/pets/
animal_shelters/
how_to_volunteer_at_
your_local_animal_shelter.html

Information about spaying and neutering:

Myths and facts:
www.peninsulahumanesociety.org/
resource/spay.html

Where to go:
www.aspca.org/pet-care/
spayneuter/

Locate dog parks in your community:
www.dogparkusa.com

Dog-related information and advice:
www.dogplay.com

Information and tips about traveling with your pet:
www.petswelcome.com

Find general pet care information:
www.healthypet.com

About the Author/Photographer

Christi Drue Dunlap lives in the San Francisco Bay Area with her husband, daughter, two dogs and two cats, all of whom are pictured in this book. Christi is a life long animal lover whose interest in advocacy and education were ignited when she joined the Animal Kindness Club in the fourth grade. She never looked back, and has always maintained an interest in helping animals.

Christi and Rocky the Pug volunteer together through the Peninsula Humane Society & SPCA's humane education program, visiting grade schools throughout the county to educate children about the needs and safety of companion animals.

A portion of the net proceeds of this book will be donated to the Peninsula Humane Society & SPCA.

Visit
www.luckymebook.com
for more information and updates!

Many photos in this book were taken at the Peninsula Humane Society & SPCA in San Mateo, CA, a private, non-profit unaffiliated with any national animal organizations which now finds homes for 100% of healthy dogs and cats in its care.

Gratitudes

This book would not have been possible without the Humane Education Program at The Peninsula Humane Society & SPCA, with which Rocky and I have had the pleasure of being affiliated. Amy D., I am forever grateful for your unwavering support. Maria D., Javan C. and Dr. Franck, thank you for your willingness to be photographed for this book. It's all the richer for you being in it.

Kik, our mutual love for animals, and constant discussion of it, brought me back to the same Humane Society we both loved as children. Thank you for your encouragement to pursue writing this book.

Tita, your humor, encouragement and help were invaluable. Seeing this as "our" project made it seem so much less overwhelming.

Lindsey, Roger, Maria E., Amanda and Thomas, thank you for lending me the faces of precious furry friends.

Also from Summerland Publishing

Are You A Good Sport? provides kids with key aspects of sportsmanship and character by using illustrations andrhymes. In a society that constantly stresses winning, "Are You A Good Sport?" allows children to see that enjoying athletics, being a team player and getting the most out of your ability are the most important things.

Wayne Soares just finished a season with his new TV show, The Sportsfan, a popular sports/comedy television program. His newest TV project is titled "All About Kids" and showcases children in a non-competitive atmosphere.
Price: $14.95   ISBN: 978-0-9795444-7-7

Have you ever contemplated how to go about explaining the concept of integrity to a five year old? Don't you wish children would have a better understanding of the core values so often eluding them in today's society, ***especially in the face of all of the unethical actions taking place in our capitol these days?*** Bud Bottoms, an internationally acclaimed sculptor of ocean life, has written a book called *Kid Ethics* that responds to this void in a child's education. Summerland Publishing has now released *Kid Ethics 2*, a follow-up to the original *Kid Ethics*, both of which can make a major impact on the world.

While *Kid Ethics* is geared towards children ages 5-10, it can be enlightening for the whole family. Mr. Bottoms takes the letters of the alphabet and assigns an ethic to each. Things like honesty, justice and open-mindedness are explained with short stories to which everyone can relate. They are accompanied by the author's pleasant illustrations that can be colored in by the reader. A two-line poem then summarizes the ethic, making it easier to digest.
Price: $17.95   ISBN: 978-0-9794863-1-9

"The Mountain Boy"by Christina Pages is a wonderful children's story about a young boy and his love of nature. The first in a series of books by author Christina Pages, this book has lovely illustrations painted by artist Jeannette Caruth, which enrich the fascinating lessons learned by the main character, Joshua. His unique ability to interact with all forms of nature is both endearing and educational for young readers. *Christina Pages is an educator and has written many great stories as well as some beautiful poetry*
Price: $15.95   ISBN: 978-0-9794863-9-5

Order Any of These Great Books From: www.summerlandpublishing.com,
www.amazon.com, www.barnesandnoble.com, or find them in your local bookstore!
Distributed through Ingram, Baker & Taylor, New Leaf & Quality Books.
Email: SummerlandPubs@aol.com for more information.
Summerland Publishing, 21 Oxford Drive, Lompoc, CA 93436   PH/Fax: (805) 735-5241